An Elephant
in my Backyard

Shobha Viswanath
Sadhvi Jawa

Every Friday, Maya and Paati
visited the temple. Maya always
carried a banana for Sangu
the temple elephant.

'Sangu, you are getting so fat!'
Maya said one Friday.

'She is going to have a baby,'
Paati said wisely.

'Oh!' Maya gasped in wonder.

Sure enough, the next Friday, when Maya went to the temple, there was a baby elephant standing next to Sangu.

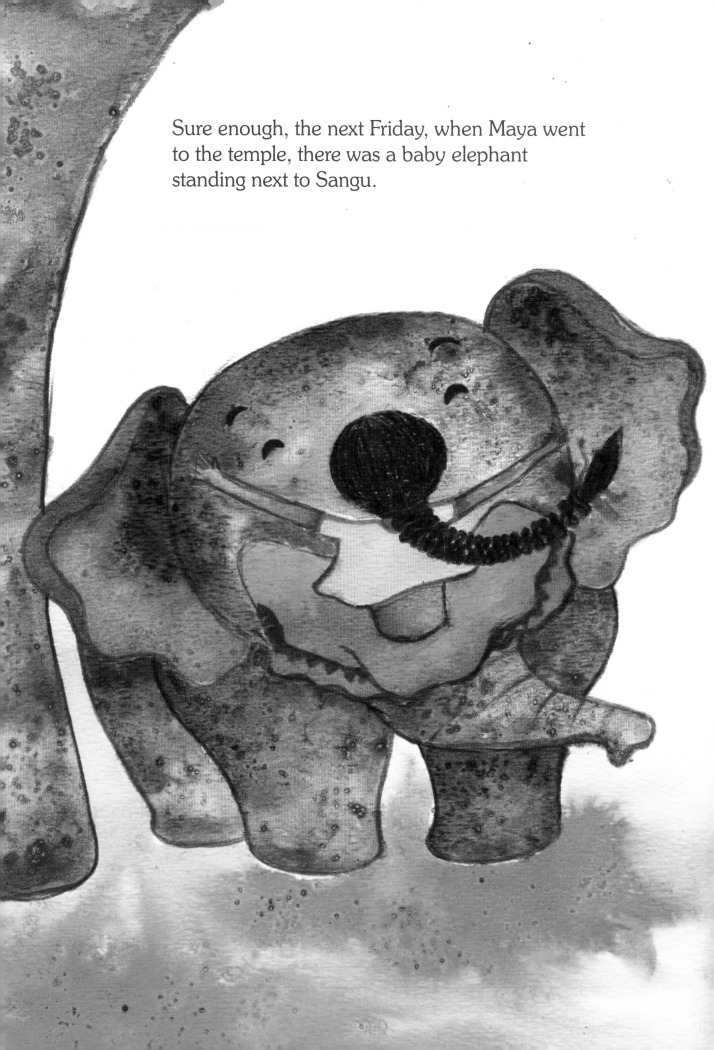

'You're the same size as me!'
Maya gushed. 'Will you come to
my home?'

'Achoooo!' the elephant sneezed.

'Bless you, Acchu!' squealed
Maya with laughter.

As Maya and Paati walked home, Maya saw that her shadow was a little larger than usual.

'Acchu!' she squealed.

'Bless you,' said Paati.

'Paati, the elephant has come home with us,'
she shouted in delight.

'Yes, dear,' said Paati, looking at the face
of Ganesha above the front door.

'Can he come inside?'

'No, let him remain outside.'

'Amma,' said Maya, 'What do baby elephants eat?'

'Fruits, coconuts, leaves and other things,' said Amma, 'They are vegetarians. Why do you ask?'

'There is an elephant in our backyard,' replied Maya.

'Of course there is,' laughed Amma. 'And there is a tiger in my tummy.'

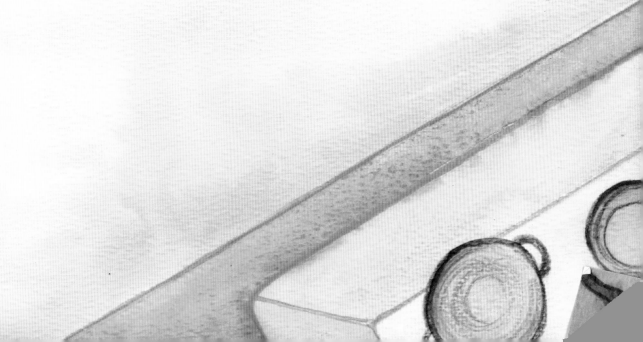

'Acchu! See what I've got for you!'

Amma caught sight
of something that looked
like a small trunk.
'Is there really an elephant
in my backyard?'
Amma wondered
and peered out.

'Oh, it is just the hosepipe!'

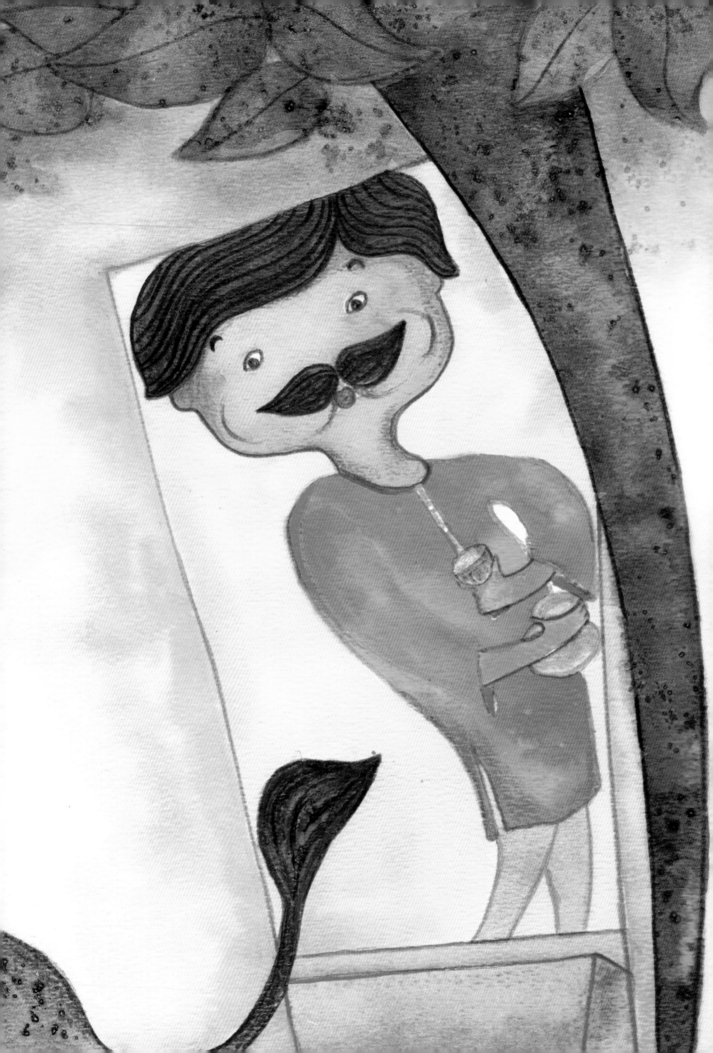

Outside, Acchu walked past the window.
'Is that an elephant in my backyard?'
Appa wondered and looked out.

'Maya, I thought you were an elephant!'

'No, that's Acchu!' Maya said.

'Bless you,' said Appa.

Just then there was a loud trumpet.

'Is there an elephant in my backyard?'
cried Paati and Thatha together.

Sangu had come in search of Acchu.
Off went Acchu, following his mother.

'Bye, Acchu!' Maya waved.

'Maya! What's this mess?'

'I told you there was an elephant
in our backyard!' said Maya,
'It was Acchu!'

'Bless you!' said Amma
and Appa and Paati and Thatha.

An Elephant in my Backyard

© and ℗ 2013 Karadi Tales Company Pvt. Ltd.

Text: Shobha Viswanath
Illustrations: Sadhvi Jawa

Karadi Tales Company Pvt. Ltd.
3A Dev Regency, 11 First Main Road, Gandhinagar, Adyar, Chennai 600 020.
Ph: +91 44 4205 4243 Email: contact@karaditales.com
Website: www.karaditales.com

Distributed in North America by Consortium Book Sales & Distribution
The Keg House 34 Thirteenth Avenue NE Suite 101 Minneapolis MN 55413-1006 USA
Orders: (+1) 731-423-1550; orderentry@perseusbooks.com
Electronic ordering via PUBNET (SAN 631760X); Website: www.cbsd.com

Printed in India
ISBN No.: 978-81-8190-240-5